DATE DUE	
MY 7 '90		
JA 1 '93		
MY 05 '95		
MY 30 '95		

BIG SIXTEEN

BIG SIXTEEN

retold by Mary Calhoun
illustrated by Trina Schart Hyman

WILLIAM MORROW AND COMPANY
New York • 1983

AUTHOR'S NOTE

Although the black folk hero Big Sixteen seems not to be generally known in the United States, his story has been told for generations in various southern states, including Florida, Georgia and Tennessee. Versions of this tale have been collected in MULES AND MEN (Zora Neale Hurston) and FOLK STORIES OF THE SOUTH (M.A. Jagendorf). I have been telling the story for many years, and through the telling my interpretation has evolved. The end of the story repeats a motif found in Appalachian folk tales, notably WICKED JOHN AND THE DEVIL (Richard Chase).

Text copyright © 1983 by Mary Calhoun
Illustrations copyright © 1983 by Trina Schart Hyman

Printed in the United States of America.

1 2 3 4 5 6 7 8 9 10

Library of Congress Cataloging in Publication Data
Calhoun, Mary.   Big Sixteen.
Summary: Big Sixteen's extra size and strength get him into trouble when The Old Man asks him to fetch the devil.
[1. Folklore, Afro-American] I. Hyman, Trina Schart, ill. II. Title.   PZ8.1.C156Bi 1983 398.2′1′08996073 [E] 83-1007
ISBN 0-688-02350-9
ISBN 0-688-02351-7 (lib. bdg.)

To Copper,
In memory of storytelling

Now, Big Sixteen was his name, 'cause that was the size
of his shoe! This was back in slavery times, when Big Sixteen
worked for The Old Man. And Big Sixteen was so big and so
strong that The Old Man thought he could do anything,
fetch anything.

One time The Old Man said, "Big Sixteen, I want you to go down in the swamp and fetch me up some cypress sills."

"Why, yassuh," said Big Sixteen.

He went on down to the swamp, where some cypress trees had been sawed up into twelve-by-twelve timbers. That's the heaviest wood there is. But Big Sixteen picked up one load of twelve-by-twelves under one arm. And he picked up another load of twelve-by-twelves under the other arm. And he brought 'em on up to the house. Ain't no man been able to do that, before nor since.

Another time The Old Man said, "Big Sixteen, I want you to go down in the pasture and fetch me up them mules."

"Why, yassuh," said Big Sixteen.

And he went on down to the pasture. Now, they were two of the tee-balkiest mules in the county. They had halters on 'em, so Big Sixteen took ahold of the halters, and he pulled. And the mules hauled, and he pulled, and they hauled, until they had pulled them halters all to pieces.

So Big Sixteen picked up one mule and put it under one arm. He picked up the other mule and put it under the other arm. And he brought 'em on up to the house.

"I law, Big Sixteen!" said The Old Man. "You are so big and so strong, I b'lieve you could fetch anything. I b'lieve you could fetch me the Devil himself!"

"Why, yassuh," said Big Sixteen, "if'n you get me a big pick and a big shovel and a nine-pound hammer."

So The Old Man sent for them things.

And Big Sixteen started in to dig a hole out in the side yard. He picked and he shoveled on that hole for thirty days, until he got down to where he was goin' to. He took that nine-pound hammer, and he stepped on out into Hell.

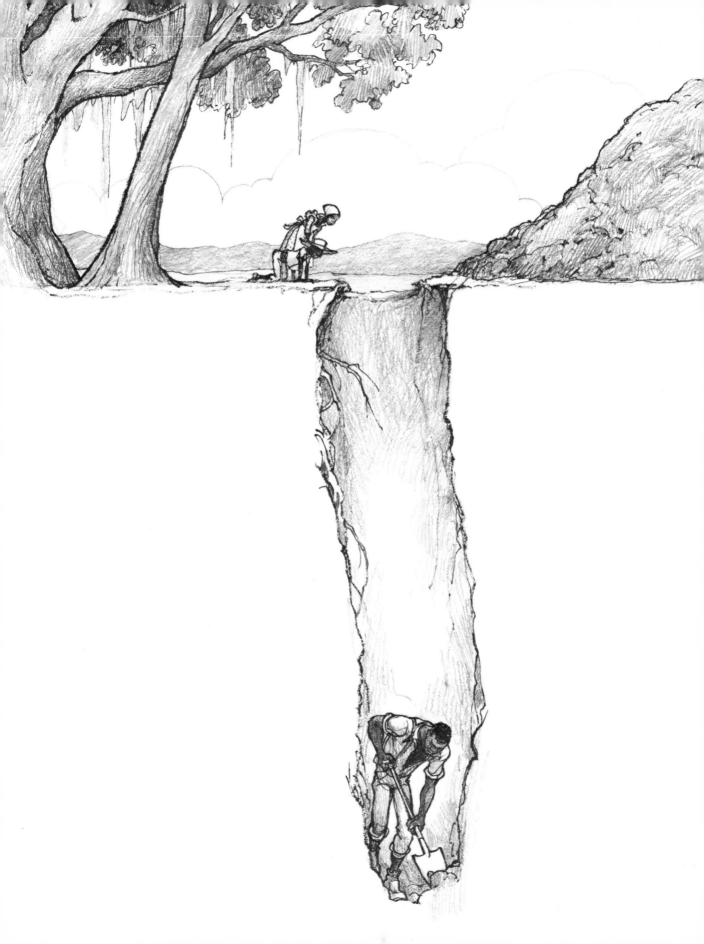

The Devil's children were playin' out in the dooryard. When they saw that big black man a-comin', they run for the house, cryin', "Mama, Mama!" The Devil's wife grabbed them children into the house and slammed the door.

Big Sixteen walked on up to the door, and he knocked on the door with the hammer, *blam, blam.*

The old Devil himself was inside. "Who's that out there?"

"It's Big Sixteen."

"What you want?"

"I wanta see you."

The Devil opened the door, poked his head out… and Big Sixteen hit 'im over the head with the nine-pound hammer, *blam!* Kilt that old Devil dead.

Then Big Sixteen took the Devil under one arm, and he climbed back up the hole. He walked into The Old Man's house and threw the Devil down on the front room floor.

"I law, Big Sixteen!" cried The Old Man. "I didn't *really* b'lieve you'd fetch me the Devil. Oh, he is so ugly! Get 'im out of here! We are gonna be sweepin' up ugly for days!"

"Why, yassuh," said Big Sixteen. And he took the ugly old Devil out and dropped 'im back down the hole.

Well, Big Sixteen lived out his good long life, and at last he died and went up to Heaven.

Saint Peter was standin' there at the pearly gates. When he saw that big black man a-comin', he said, "Now, hold on there. You can't come in."

"And why not?" said Big Sixteen. "I done lived a good clean life!"

"Oh, I know that," said Saint Peter, kinda squirmin'.
"I know you have. But the trouble is, you are so big and
strong, if you got outta hand, there ain't nobody up here
could handle you. So you better go on to some other
place."

"Why, yassuh," said Big Sixteen, disgusted-like. And he
went on down to Hell.

The Devil's children were still playin' out in the dooryard. When they saw Big Sixteen a-comin', they run for the house, cryin', "Mama, Mama, here come that man what kilt Papa!"

The Devil's wife grabbed the children into the house and slammed the door.

Big Sixteen just walked on up to the door. *Knock, knock.*
Devil's wife called out, "What you want?"

"I wanta come in."

There was a long wait. Then the door opened just a tee-ninchy crack, and the Devil's wife stuck her hand out. In her hand was a hot flaming coal.

"You can't come in! But here's a little piece of fire. Now you go start a hell of your own!"

And so, if you ever see a light flickerin' down in the swamp at night, or a light movin' around in the woods, you know it's Big Sixteen, with his little piece of fire, a-lookin' for a place to go.